W9-BSH-251

FOR LIZA, WHO BELIEVES IN DREAMS TOO.

Library of Congress Cataloging-in-Publication Data

Boyd, Lizi, 1953-
Inside outside / by Lizi Boyd.
p. cm.
Images from the following pages appear through die-cut holes, for example, a plant outside becomes a plant in a vase.
Summary: In this story without words, a boy and his dog play inside and outside of their home.
ISBN 978-1-4521-0644-1 (alk. paper)

1. Dogs—Juvenile fiction. 2. Play—Juvenile fiction. 3. Toy and movable books—Specimens. 4. Board books.
[1. Dogs—Fiction. 2. Play—Fiction. 3. Stories without words. 4. Toy and movable books. 5. Board books.] I. Title.

PZ7.B6924Ins 2012
[E]—dc23

2012015430

Design by Lizi Boyd and Sara Gillingham Studio.
Typeset in Oyster and Potato Cut.
The illustrations in this book were painted in gouache on kraft paper.

Manufactured in China.

10 9 8 7 6 5 4 3 2

Chronicle Books LLC
680 Second Street, San Francisco, California 94107

www.chroniclekids.com

INSIDE OUTSIDE

LIZI BOYD

chronicle books · san francisco

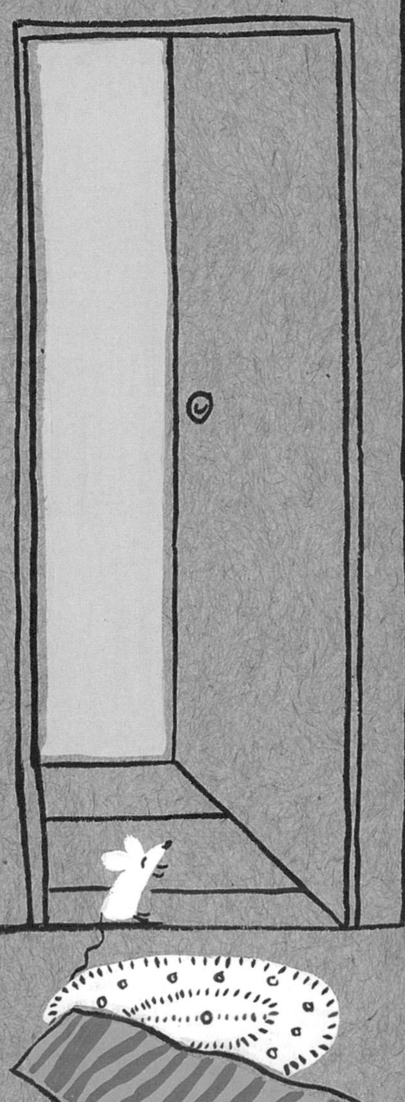

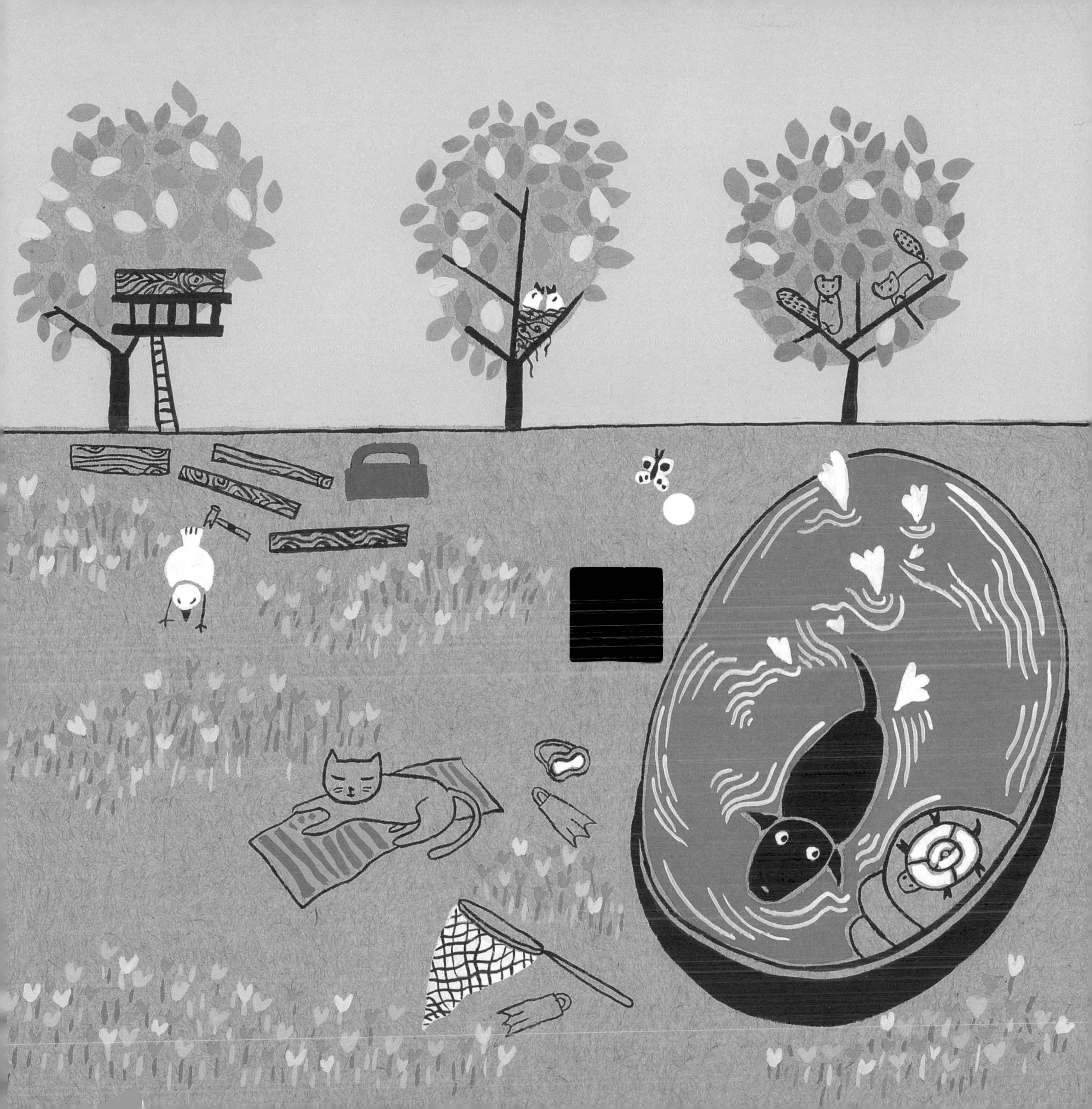